Cows on the Farm

by Mari C. Schuh

Holstein cow

Consulting Editor: Gail Saunders-Smith, Ph.D.

Consultant: Donna Lange
Communication Programs Coordinator
Dairy Farmers of Ontario
Mississauga, Ontario

Pebble Books

an imprint of Capstone Press
Mankato, Minnesota

Pebble Books are published by Capstone Press,
1710 Roe Crest Drive, North Mankato, Minnesota 56003.
www.capstonepub.com

Library of Congress Cataloging-in-Publication Data
Schuh, Mari C., 1975–
    Cows on the farm / by Mari C. Schuh.
    p. cm.—(On the farm.)
    Includes bibliographical references (p. 23) and index.
    ISBN-13: 978-0-7368-0992-4 (hardcover)
    ISBN-10: 0-7368-0992-9 (hardcover)
    ISBN-13: 978-0-7368-9143-1 (softcover pbk.)
    ISBN-10: 0-7368-9143-9 (softcover pbk.)
    1. Cows—Juvenile literature. [1. Cows.] I. Title. II. Series.
SF197.5 .S38 2002
636.2—dc21   2001000467

Summary: Simple text and photographs present cows and how they are raised.

Note to Parents and Teachers

The series On the Farm supports national science standards related
to life science. This book describes and illustrates cows on the
farm. The photographs support early readers in understanding the
text. The repetition of words and phrases helps early readers learn
new words. This book also introduces early readers to subject-
specific vocabulary words, which are defined in the Words to Know
section. Early readers may need assistance to read some words and
to use the Table of Contents, Words to Know, Read More, Internet
Sites, and Index/Word List sections of the book.

Printed in the United States of America in North Mankato, Minnesota.
022014   008009R

Table of Contents

ears

udder

legs

hooves

Cows live on farms.

Jersey cow

Some farmers raise cows
for their meat.

Black Angus and Charolais cows

Some farmers raise cows for their milk. Farmers milk cows with machines.

Holstein cow

Veterinarians help
keep cows healthy.

Jersey cow and calf

Cows live in barns most of the winter.

Red Holstein cow

Farmers feed hay
and grain to cows.

Holstein cows

Cows graze in pastures.
They eat grass.

Holstein cows

Cows chew their cud.

Holstein cow

20

Cows moo.

Brown Swiss cow

Words to Know

barn—a building where animals, crops, and small pieces of equipment are kept

cud—food that has not been fully digested; cows bring up food from their stomach to chew again; then they swallow the food after it has been chewed again.

machine—a piece of equipment made of moving parts that is used to do a job

pasture—land that animals use to graze; to graze means to eat grass or other plants that are growing in a pasture or field.

raise—to care for animals as they grow and become older; some farmers raise cows for their meat; some farmers raise cows for their milk; people use cows' milk to make cheese and other products.

veterinarian—a doctor who treats sick or injured animals; veterinarians also check animals to make sure they are healthy.

Read More

Bell, Rachael. *Cows.* Farm Animals. Chicago: Heinemann Library, 2000.

Miller, Sara Swan. *Cows.* A True Book. New York: Children's Press, 2000.

Stone, Lynn M. *Cows Have Calves.* Animals and Their Young. Minneapolis: Compass Point Books, 2000.

Internet Sites

FactHound offers a safe, fun way to find Internet sites related to this book. All of the sites on FactHound have been researched by our staff.

Here's all you do:

Visit *www.facthound.com*

FactHound will fetch the best sites for you!

Index/Word List

barns, 13	grass, 17	milk, 9
chew, 19	graze, 17	moo, 21
cud, 19	hay, 15	most, 13
eat, 17	healthy, 11	pastures, 17
farmers, 7, 9, 15	help, 11	raise, 7, 9
farms, 5	keep, 11	some, 7, 9
feed, 15	live, 5, 13	veterinarians, 11
grain, 15	machines, 9	winter, 13
	meat, 7	

Word Count: 56
Early-Intervention Level: 8

Credits

Heather Kindseth, cover designer; Heidi Meyer, production designer; Kimberly Danger and Deirdre Barton, photo researchers

Capstone Press/Gary Sundermeyer, 6, 8
Craig Nelson/Pictor, 20
David F. Clobes, Stock Photography, 12, 14
PhotoDisc, Inc., cover
Photri-Microstock, 10
Unicorn Stock Photos/Andre Jenny, 16; Martin R. Jones, 18
Visuals Unlimited/Cheryl Jones, 1; Inga Spence, 4

Special thanks to Vicki Fleming and Adam and Jason Berndt, all of Elysian, Minnesota, for their assistance with this book.